Happy Cat First Readers

David's had a party invitation.
It's a fancy dress party
and he's going to go as a
fox. But when he arrives he
can see he's made a mistake in
hoosing his costume. Luckily, he
ıas a clever idea about how a
fox can still fit in with the
party theme while they all
have fun.

Happy Cat First Readers

Pop-Up Fox

Janeen
Brian

Illustrated by
Beth Norling

HAPPY CAT BOOKS

To Rory, who was the first fox.
Love Janeen.

To Super Sara, dress-up queen,
and to the second generation of
dress-uppers, Thom, Dan, Indigo
and Juno. *B.N.*

Published by
Happy Cat Boo
An imprint of (
Islington Busii
3-5 Islington H
London N1 9L(

First published

This edition first published 2007
1 3 5 7 9 10 8 6 4 2

Text copyright © Janeen Brian, 2004
Illustrations copyright © Beth Norling, 2004

The moral rights of the author and illustrator have been
asserted

A CIP catalogue record for this book is available from the
British Library

ISBN   978-1-905117-38-3

Printed in Poland

www.catnippublishing.co.uk

Chapter 1

'Mum, I've finished my mask!' David put on the lion mask and ran into the sewing room. 'Grrr!' he growled.

'Eeek!' cried Mum. 'Did you have lion-porridge for breakfast?'

'Yep! And lion-toast!'
David laughed. He liked
the way his mum made
jokes. 'Do you like my
mask?'

'It's great. You did a really good job.'

David smiled and padded back to his bedroom. He felt strong like a lion. He prowled around the bed with big, slow steps. He stretched his big hand-claws. He gave another growl. Baxter barked and dashed out of the room.

David decided to make a lion tail as well.

It was easy. He stuffed
an old stocking with paper
and pinned it to his shorts.
Then he lay on the floor
and opened his *favourite*

book. It was about animals.
It had the best pop-up
pictures! David always
liked pictures more than
words. Letters tripped

him up. When he said the wrong words at school, his face went pink and some kids called him a baby.

Other kids teased him about dressing up as animals too. But that didn't upset him. Not nearly as much.

Chapter 2

David wore his lion outfit
for the rest of the day. And
the next day too. He wore it
when he took Baxter for a
walk. He wore it when he
visited his old gran in the
big house with all the other
old grans. He wore it when

he bounced on the
trampoline. And he wore
it to bed.

The lion outfit made
David feel strong and
clever.

On Monday, David

dragged on his school

clothes. He ate his

breakfast, letting milk slop

from his spoon. He wished

he could wear his lion outfit

to school. Maybe then he'd
be able to read words the
right way. Maybe then
someone would think
he was clever and be
his friend.

He didn't think he'd get
an invitation to a party
that day. But that's just
what happened!

It was from the new boy.
He'd said, 'You have to
come dressed as something

that starts with the same
letter as my name.'

'Thanks,' said David,
wide-eyed.

After school, he rushed home and yelled, 'Mum! Guess what!'

'I'm in the sewing room,' called Mum.

David ran in, panting.

'I got an invitation to a party!'

'Wow. Who from?'

'That new boy I told you

about. He's only asked *four*
kids in the *whole* class. And
I'm one of them!'

'That's great, David.
When's the party?'

'This Saturday. And, guess what? It's a fancy dress party!'

'Oh. You can wear your lion outfit then.'

'No, I can't. You can't just dress up as *anything*, Mum. You have to wear something that...'

The phone rang. 'Hang on,' said Mum. 'That will be the shop about those curtains I'm making.

You think about what you'd
like to take as a present.
Then you can tell me about
it later.'

Chapter 3

That night David lay in
bed, hands behind his head.
What could he go to the
party as? He had to dress
up as something that began
with the letter *f*.

The moon shone through
the window and made

shapes and shadows on the
wall. If he squinted a bit,
David could see the shape
of something strange. It
had a pointed nose and two
stiff ears. David gasped.

Now he knew what he'd go as!

Next morning he was still excited. He dressed quickly and gobbled his breakfast. At school, Sashi, Max and

Kim were sitting on the
seats under the trees.
They were going to the
party too.

Sashi waved. 'Come over
here!' she called.

David's heart thumped.
He'd never been real
friends with them before.
He ran up.

'Do you know what you're
going as?' said Sashi.

David went to speak.

'Don't tell us!' cried Max.

David went pink.

Max looked at the others.

'None of us are telling.'

'We're just giving a clue,' said Sashi.

'Then you can see if you guessed right at the party!' said Kim with a smile.

'Oh,' said David. 'Do I say a clue?'

The others all nodded. David felt better. 'I'm going as an animal,' he said.

No one said anything. David shuffled his feet.

Then Sashi said, 'I'm

going as something from
the sea.'

Maybe she'll be a *fish*,
thought David.

'I'm going as something
that you eat,' said Kim.

Could be *fruit*, thought
David.

'I'm going as something that flies,' said Max. 'But not a bird.'

The bell rang. They all ran to their classroom.

Much later, David thought that Max might go as a *frisbee*!

Chapter 4

David couldn't wait to start
his new mask. He opened
his animal book at the right
page and then set out
everything he needed.

First, he folded a piece of
cardboard to make a cone.
He made it very pointy!

Then he coloured in the face
and cut holes for the eyes
and mouth. Finally, he taped
on two cardboard ears and

some whiskers, and tied
elastic at the back. At last he
was finished. David smiled
and slipped on the mask.

Then he crept quietly into the lounge. His dad was doing a crossword.

'GGGRRRRR!' David yelled and pounced.

'Yikes!' His dad's pen flew in the air.

David burst out laughing.

'I thought you were real,' said Dad.

'I am,' said David and laughed again. 'Where's Mum?'

'In the kitchen,' came
a voice.

'Mum, I need something
good to make a fox tail
with. Can you help me?'

His mum found a bit of
brown, fluffy material.

David cut it and pinned it
to a brown jumper. Then
he put on black tracksuit
trousers. He found some old
black gloves for paws. With
his mask on as well, he

really felt like a fox, strong
and sly and clever.

'Looks good, Davey,' said
Dad. 'Where's the party?'

'I don't know,' said David

behind the mask. 'I'll get
the invitation.' But when he
got to his room, there was
Baxter. He was sniffing in

David's school bag for food
scraps. On the floor was
the invitation, torn and
chewed.

'Baxter!' cried David.

The dog stared, then shot out of the room.

'I can *just* read the address,' said Dad, when David handed him the scrap of paper.

Chapter 5

The next day was party day. David couldn't wait. When he was ready, Mum took a photo.

'Have you got the present?' said Dad.

David nodded. It was a book. The same pop-up

animal book that he had!

David climbed in the car

and then gave a cry.

'What's wrong?' said Dad.

'I just sat on my tail!'

Both David and his dad
laughed.

Soon, David's dad turned
the car into a long street.
David saw balloons flying
in the air. They were tied to
a gate.

'That must be the house!'
cried David.

Not long after, David's
dad knocked on the door.

A lady answered. 'Hello,'
she said.

'Hello. This is my son, David.'

'Hi,' said the lady. 'Come in, David. The others are in the back room.'

'I'll pick you up at four o'clock,' said Dad, waving goodbye.

David walked down the hall, smiling. He couldn't wait to see what the other kids were wearing. Had he guessed right about their costumes?

In the back room, the other children were looking at the presents.

'Hi,' they all said.

'Hello,' said David, but he was puzzled. Sashi wasn't a fish. She was a pirate. Kim wasn't dressed as fruit. He was a pizza. And Max wasn't a frisbee. He was a plane.

David frowned. The others stared at him too.

'What animal are you?'
said Sashi.

David took a breath. 'I'm
a . . . a . . . fox.' But his
tummy felt lumpy.

Something was wrong. He

didn't know what it was.

'A *fox*?' said Max and

looked at the others. 'But

that starts with *f*.'

What was the matter
with that? thought David.
He knew *fox* started with *f*.
He knew he had to dress-up
in something that had the
same starting letter as the
name of the birthday boy.
So what was wrong?

'My name starts with *p*,'
said Philip. 'Didn't you
know?'

David stood as if he were
pinned to the floor. He

hadn't seen Philip's name
written on the invitation
because Baxter had made a
mess of it. Now he'd done
something really stupid.

David looked at the kids
again and his heart sank.
Philip was dressed as a
penguin. The others were

wearing something that
started with *p* as well.
A pirate, a pizza and a plane.
David's face went pink.

His heart beat hard.

'It's okay,' said Philip.
'I don't mind. It's a silly
name anyway.'

'Could you be another
animal?' said Sashi.
'Something that starts
with *p*?'

David bit his lip. How
could he be? He had a fox
mask, a fox tail and fox
paws. A fox *couldn't* be
another animal.

'I know!' cried Max. 'You could still be a fox, but you could be a Party Fox.'

'Or, a Pretend Fox,' said Sashi.

'Or, a Papa Fox,' said
Kim. 'That'd be all right,
wouldn't it, Philip?'
'Yeah.'

David shook his head. He couldn't be a Papa Fox because he was a baby. And he was a baby because he didn't know proper letters! David spun around. He started to run . . . but he tripped over his fox tail.

Chapter 6

He came down on the floor
with a hard bump. He felt
so bad. He wanted to just
stay there and cry. But
when he looked at the
birthday present still in
his hands, David had
a wonderful idea. With a

small sniff, he said, 'Philip,
could I be . . . could I be . . .
a *Pop-up Fox*?'

'What do you mean?'

'Like this.' David did a
HUGE jump!

'Wow. *That's* a good Pop-
up Fox!' laughed Philip.

Sashi, Kim and Max
laughed too.

'A Pop-up Fox is funny,'
said Kim.

'Yeah. And it starts with
p,' said Max.

'Pop-up Foxes have to

chase you!' shouted Sashi.
She ran out through the
doorway and into the
backyard.

'Yeah!' yelled the others.
They ran outside as well.

'Look out!' cried David and raced after them.

'Chase me, Pop-up Fox!' called Kim.

'Can't catch me!' screamed Philip.

'Or me!'

'Or me!'

David chased the kids around and around the garden. Max's wings flapped. Kim's pizza outfit wobbled. Sashi's eye-patch

fell off and Philip's beak
flapped in his face. David
caught him easily. The fox
and the penguin tumbled
over and over, laughing.

After the games, Philip's
mum put the party food
on the table. There was
so much to choose from.
There were little pies and
pasties, pikelets, popcorn,

pineapple jelly and party
cakes!

Four o'clock came too
quickly.

Chapter 7

There was a scramble to
the door when the bell
rang. David's dad was first.
David said goodbye and
thanked Philip's mum.

'Got everything?' she said.

David looked at what he
was carrying. There was

the bag of lollies, the piece
of birthday cake, the fox
mask, the fox tail and the
gloves. He nodded.

Once they were in the
car, Dad said, 'How was the
party, Davey?'

David smiled. His eyes
shone. 'It was great!' he said.

On the way home, David's smile grew bigger. The party *had* been fun, but now there was something else to look forward to. On Monday he'd go back to school and Philip would be there. Philip was his friend.

And David knew *that* started with *f*!

From Janeen Brian

My nephew in New Zealand once had a fox costume. He not only loved it, but felt he *was* a fox when he wore it. Then, when my daughter, Cassie, had a 21st birthday party, she asked all her friends to come dressed as something starting with the letter *c*. I used those two memories, along with some imagination, to come up with the story idea of *Pop-up Fox*.

From Beth Norling

I loved dressing up. I was Bionic Beth and my best friend was a super hero too. Super Sara had her initials cut out in paper and pinned to her super-hero outfit. I was wearing my underwear on the outside. Together, from the swing set in her backyard, we would go forth and save the world!

We were invincible . . .

The Princess
and the Unicorn

Wendy Blaxland

No one believes in unicorns any more. Except Princess Lily, that is.
So when the king falls ill and the only thing that can cure him is
the magic of a unicorn, it's up to her to find one.
But can Lily find a magical unicorn in time?

When Anna
Slept Over

Jane Godwin

Josie is Anna's best friend. Anna has played at Josie's house,
she's even stayed for dinner, but she has never slept over.
Until now...

The Magic Wand

Ursula Dubosarsky

Becky was cross with her little brother. 'If you don't leave me alone,' she said to him, 'I'll put a spell on you!' But she didn't mean to make him disappear!

The Gorilla Suit

Victor Kelleher

Tom was given a gorilla suit for his birthday. He loved it and wore it everywhere. When mum and dad took him to the zoo he wouldn't wear his ordinary clothes. But isn't it asking for trouble to go to the zoo dressed as a gorilla?

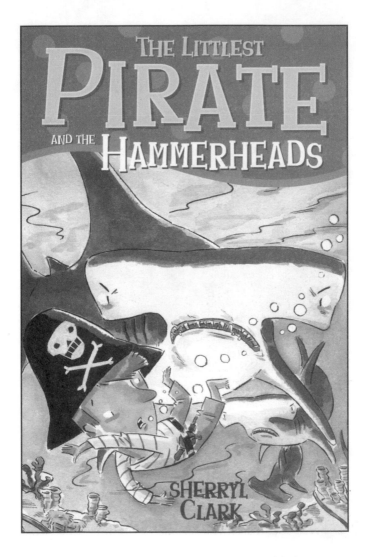

Nicholas Nosh, the littlest pirate in the world, has to rescue his family's treasure which has been stolen by Captain Hammerhead. But how can he outwit the sharks that are guarding Captain Hammerhead's ship?

Crystal longs to be a mermaid.
Her mother makes her a flashing silver tail. But it isn't like
being a proper mermaid. Then one night Crystal wears her
tail to bed...

First day at new school for Kerry.
It's easy to get lost in a big new school when you don't
know anyone. But a helpful dog shows Kerry the way to the
playground - and to lots of new friends!

Jock can make a special sound like a duck!
If you can learn to make it too you can help Jock rescue the
little duck from the duck hunter. Quick, before it's too late!